FUNNY KID

SO, THIS PARTICULAR BOOK IS ABOUT A PARTICULAR KID WHOSE LIFE WAS WEIRD AND PRETTY FUNNY AND EVERYTHING AWKWARD AND HAPPENED TO HIM

ADARSH AGRAWAL

To my freinds

Contents

PREFACE

So, this is a fictional book and i t has a story about a weird funny kid. This story is was written by me when I was 14 years old. Its very interesting story and you will laugh as much as your stomach will start hurting.

This is very interesting book for children you will not feel boring anytime. When you would be reading thi story you will be feeling that the scenario of the whole story is happening infront of your eyes. And you will surely laugh out loud.

- The author (Adarsh Agrawal)

I

THE FIRST CLASS

After kindergarden, when I was ready for primary school and my age was enough my mom sent me school by driving our old van and actually you all would be thinking I would be very happy to go to school, but this was not the truth in reality i was not at all happy I was weeping like an kid whoses lollipop has been stolen by man and who has been punched in his face so, this was my condition.

After a while my mom was trying to encourage me up in the van and she told that your first day of primary school would go very smooth but actualy I had heard about it from my brother pringles that first of school was pretty

damn hilarious evrything would go very funny and weird you would cry like every second in the school.

So when I reached school I saw many buses and many cars. And then my mom took me to school and she left me with my class teacher till that time also i was weeping very much. After that teacher gave me chocolates so I stopped crying and then she guided me to the classroom to introduce my then when suddenly I arrived my classroom all of the students started laughing at me because my face was very funny and actually it was pretty much like a donkey wearing circle frames specs.

And then my teacher introduced me and then I sat on the last bench , where no one was sitting , then after the first period one kid named manchow came to me. He was very fat and chubby and he was pretty messy too. he introduced himself and in his introduction I came to know that his father was the Top 10 most richest person in the world and he was very popular and he also told that he lived in apartment with fifteen floor. He came to me for friendship because no one came to me for freindship and everyone was thinking I am damn stupid. So it was very nice for him to ask to become freinds I also felt very good then he sat with me and after one more boring class our period bell rang and this was lunch time.

In lunch time manchow introduced me about his vacation in India where he went Taj mahal in agra it was very beautiful place where there was fort made up of white marble. It was build by a king named shah jahan. Its white colour is very beautiful. It looks different in different times of day. It looks white in afternoon. oraange in sunset. And golden white in the night.

Then he told me about the second trip of saudi arabia it is a country full of rich people it is a developed country and it loads of petrol and loads of buildings structures and artificial island. And the most tallest building named burj khalifa.

Then we ate our lunch which had delicious sausage, french fries, burger, some strwberries and mango. Then I felt to pee and as a matter of fact I was eating and in the reason of embarassment in going washroom I actually peed in my fucking pants and then when evryone saw me then they told pee pee pee and everyone was making fun of me. and this moment was very embarassing and felt pretty ashamed then my friend manchow also made fun of me. then after that my freind told me'ok no problem, I can understand you can go to washroom and wash your pants and then let then dry and ask some extra pants from school authority.

As it was my first day of school and i did'nt knew that where was washroom and my peed pants were soaked with pee and every one seeing my and laughing out a lot they were staring and me and teeling me that -'go child wear you diapers' and I again started weeping and then somehow I managed to ask the way to wahroom from a girl and she told me after seeing my whole outfit.

And when I reached washroom in a hurry so to not to get seen I by mistake stepped inside girls washroom and then each girls started staring me and then I ran out of the washroom.

Then I went to boys washroom , after washing my pants I let them dry and then in my underwear I went to the office to ask any pants and then in my way the students saw me and they started making fun of me more ludly and this time it was pretty more embarassing and hilarious and when I went towards the office every single staff, parents started staring me then I asked the that if they had any pants and after that they did'nt had any pants but they had frock, so ihad to weat that frock. And in reality first of all I was looking like a boy wearing frock and second to me female teacher (Mrs. Potato) applied lipistick to me and then after a while I looked at mirror as I had face like donkey and I was looking like a donkey wearing frock and did makeup.

When I reached classroom I everyone was again laughing again. So I started weeping loudly and due that reason that same teacher came who applied lipstick and after tha my mother was called.

When my mother came and saw me in a frock she also started making fun of me and said that I was looking like her daughter And she told me Ramen how you became a girl and Then i explained her whole story then, she told me not be embarassed while going washroom and then she took me home .

II

THE STINKY CHEESE

So my day started like this my mischevious brother pringles who studied in high school woke me up by telling ramen its time for your school wake up. The after that I got up and then I saw the clock it was 6 a:m and my school timing was 6:30 a:m and my bus timing was 6:15 . As i saw the timing I jumped up from my bed then ran towards washroom which was actually closed because my grandfather was inside and sound was coming like this -pt.....tptppptptptt whoosh.

After that I screamed from outside -"grandpa I have to brush come out" then he told wait I have noodles stuck in my stomach and I have to get it all out and then I agreed. and then he came out then I hurreidly walked into the washroom took my brush and then satrted brushing my teeth fastly then After 30.01 sec I started bathing and then suddenly green colour came out of my shower and I was covered in green colour and I looked like a zombie pig and then when green colour stopped coming out and water was sputtering out of it and again to remove that green colour i started bathing and still some colour was left on my body but that was not that much noticable and then after that I dried myself then I went to kitchen

. But I knew who has done the job of putting green coulour in the shower and it was my bloody brother pringles who disturbed me and bullied me from my childhood.

And in kitchen I took cornflakes and then took milk hurriedly but I did'nt care and I ignored as I had to go to school I ate the breakfast and then suddenly my dad came and asked me what I was doing I told that I was getting ready for school. And the he told me if i was mad it was 4 ., your school is at 6:30 you should ggo sleep. I told him Pringles has told me that it is 6:30. He said "ok now enough ,go and sleep peacefully".

I became very angry on Pringles and decided that one day I would take revenge from him because he tricked me badly and I came to know that he changed my clock timing and the alarm and then again I went to sleep.

Then when I woke up with a pleasant dream after that I got up from my bed and wore school uniform and after that as I have brushed already then I went toward kitchen where my mom was preaparing tasty cheese paneer (cottage cheese) sandwiches for me and after that sat on my table and then my mom started scolding me for spilling milk on the dining table and this was not a god thing then I told her everything about today incident and explained her everything and the she called up Pringles and after that she scolded her badly and I was enjoying and laughing too much from inside after a while when the sandwiches were ready mom served us and I and Pringles went to buses.

And then I sat beside my only best freind manchow, who told me about how he ate a piece of largest fish grilled In slow griller and which was spiced up with chilli from india, garlic special sauce from mexico and 120 years old cheese from italy and the most expensive oil made from mushroom and some white truffles garnished on top of the dish and coated with the 24 carat gold foil and served in golden plate.

He told that this was the most delicious dish he has ever had. And after that he told me that you were pretty messy on that day brother.Every body was laughing on you.

After some time of chatting, we reached school i took my bag and when manchow took his bag his heavy loaded bag striked me and after that I felt as if someone stabbed me in my whole head, but after some time the pain was gone and i felt quite relieved.

After that we reached then after the same boring class on this day we had fitness period and I and manchow were both bad in this I was pretty thin like a pin andd he was too fat as a elephant and we had to run 10 rounds of 100 metres ground so in this I ran 5 rounds and Manchow ran only 2 rounds and everyone completed all the 10 rounds except us. and the same they were making fun of me and

Manchow.

After that we had to play football and we were divided in two teams and we and Manchow were both in the same teams and we were happy for that but as we both were bad in sports so we knew that our teams would surely lose and as predicted our teams lost and after that every single student started quarelling and bullied us becuase we both played very bad in the match and then on the ground I saw something very disgusting and smelly on footlball ground and then I told about it to Manchow and the we and Manchow went towards it and after that One boy came.

He introduce us and from that introduction we came to know that his name was mr. cucumber , he belonged to south indian family in India and his father who was a famouls celebrity named King mango Khan and he was a pretty genius kid who had information about almost everyone and then he told us not to touch that fucking cheese it was not good because there was a rumour about that weird stinky cheeses that who so ever touches that cheese would get cursed and mysterious and horror things would happen to him afterwards and after then he would be murdered badly and mercilessy and his whole family would get killed and his house would catch fire.

And it is pretty scary isn't it. Then after that the boy cucumber told us about one boy named Lemon who touched the cheese and after that the boy and his body was nowwhere to be found and family was also lost everyone tried to contact them but they were gone.

And from that time no one ever dared to touch this stinky old cursed cheese. This piece of sliced cheese which has pretty much fungus on it must be 500 years old and maybe it was cursed by a gypsy.

III

THE CRUSH

After eating my dinner I went to sleep and I slept I started dreaming about a pretty, dashing and beautiful girl whom I loved we were both together each and every time and we were sitting in a park and talking to each other and dicussing funny things we were in serious love with each other and then when I asked her about her that "Do you love me" actually I kind of love you very much. And she started smiling and then she was saying I .. and then suddenly my mom woke me up as it was time for going to school so i woke up and got ready for school.

After that I when I became fresh and had my breakfast and was waiting for my bus then when the bus arrived I sat beside Manchow as usual and then after that I told evrerything

about the dream to rowley and explained everything to him he told me that maybe it was my destiny that the same girl exists in real life and it is god's wish so that you both can love each other and he also told that his has did a course about seeing fortunes and destiny and luck and she told this thing to him.

After that we reached school and then we had the same boring period and then I saw that same girl in the school who was of my age and I was extremely shocked about it I thought i was day dreaming and then I asked my freind manchow to slap me so that I can know if I am not dreaming.

Then I told about it to manchow and he was also very shocked but he told me that go and talk to that girl maybe its reality and god showed you future and after that we went to classroom. Then after the both periods as usual they were pretty boring we had lunch.

And then I and Manchow and Cucumber were sitting at a chair and eating our lunch and then I and manchow explained everything about what happened today. And then he told that my father always says that god shows future to some extraordinary people and they are very lucky in their future.

And then he told that maybe he knew that girl she belonged to upper middle class family her father was famous dentist mr. Brinjal and her mother was a reknowed writed Mrs. Tomato and girl's name was Lady Finger.

And then he told that she is very popular girl and she as she is beautiful about 100s of boys have proposed her but due to some reason she has rejected them all and she is in the journey or a way to to finf out her true love and he futher tolf that maybe Ramen it was you who would be her partner in coming time.

Then after that Cucumber and Manchow encouraged him to talk to Lady finger and try to impress her. And further addding on cucumber told him that maybe it was his glimpse of his previous life and he should make that girl recall about it. and then further he was accompanied with manchow that yes he agrees with the statement of cucumber .

And after that I went to her table where she was eating alone and said 'hii' - "I am ramen" and then she said her name and after that I discussed about films, songs, comics. And then we started joking with each other and after that we became best freinds and she told me never to break freindship.

After that I told her about my dream and told that maybe we were in love with each other in our previous life and we might have forget each other and I also told her what Manchow told about destiny and also what Cucumber told and then I asked if she loved me and then she replied actually Ramen I really love you I felt in love with you on the first day itself on seeing your innocent an funny acts you are however very funny and I actually truly love you.

THE END.

Thanks for reading this book I am very grateful for this, hope you like my other books when I publish it in future

-Thank You(the author-Adarsh agrawal).

9 798887 178325

Printed by Libri Plureos GmbH in Hamburg, Germany